Pocket Watch Portal

By MM Myers

Dedication

For my children and grands, Faith, William, Emma, Jonathan, Justice, Teddy, Hope, Ellie, Samantha, and baby Artie.

Our adventure begins in a cozy little town in South Texas called Moore, where the grandparents of Justice, Teddy, Ellie, and baby Artie live.

Justice asked his Grandma whether they could go ride their cars.

It was really pretty and sunny that day, not nasty like yesterday with all the mud rain.
Ellie said, "Yeah, that was really bad. Grandma, can I go, too?"

Grandma yelled back to take baby Artie. "He wants to play, also."

Teddy came in and asked, "Baby Artie wants to go for a wagon ride."

As the kids played outside, baby Artie
started yelling, "Stop."

"What's wrong?" Teddy asked.

Artie pointed over to something very shiny.

"What on earth is that?" Justice, the eldest, saw and ran over. Ellie followed him.

"What is it?" Everybody looked at the watch.

"Wow," said Justice, "It looks like it's an old pocket watch," he said to the others.

That pocket watch just glistened in the sunlight and seemed to whisper secrets of the past and future.

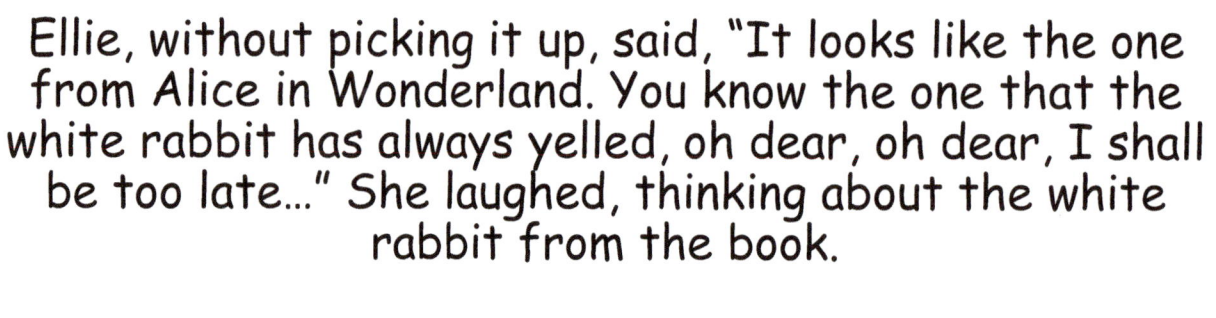

Ellie, without picking it up, said, "It looks like the one from Alice in Wonderland. You know the one that the white rabbit has always yelled, oh dear, oh dear, I shall be too late..." She laughed, thinking about the white rabbit from the book.

Curiosity piqued, and Justice picked up the pocket watch, and a magical portal suddenly appeared before them. They couldn't believe their eyes...what was going on?

Without hesitation, Justice, Teddy, Ellie, and even baby Artie stepped into the portal and found themselves in a different time.

They looked around at their surroundings, realizing they had traveled back to the time of none other than dinosaurs!

Teddy looked at Justice, and both yelled, "Dinosaurs!" With a big smile on their face.

Ellie was not so sure of what was going on.

"Dinosaurs?"

As they explored this prehistoric world, they encountered a friendly dinosaur named Dino, who had never seen humans before.

Teddy said, "That's ok. I've never met a real dinosaur before, either."

They both laughed. Dino was a gentle giant with bright green scales and a kind heart. The children quickly became friends with Dino and embarked on a thrilling adventure together.

They explored with Dino the lush jungles, crossed vast rivers, and even witnessed a T-Rex chasing its prey.

Just then, Justice stopped his younger sister and brothers, "We have got to be careful. Don't anyone let baby Artie out of sight because we better not let anything happen to him, especially don't let any dinosaur eat baby Artie, or we are all toast!"

"Got it," he said.

Along the way, they learned about different species of dinosaurs, their habitats, and the importance of preserving nature.

"Wow, Dino, this place is incredible!" exclaimed Teddy, his eyes wide with excitement. "You're right, Teddy! Imagine what life was like when dinosaurs roamed the Earth," replied Justice, marveling at the towering creatures.

Ellie, with her vivid imagination, added, "I bet they had so many fascinating adventures just like we do!"

As they continued their journey, the children noticed a baby dinosaur trapped in a deep ravine. Without hesitation, Justice, Teddy, and Ellie worked together to rescue the poor little dinosaur, using a very strong vine and their quick wit.

"Thank you so much for saving me!" squeaked the baby dinosaur, his eyes filled with gratitude.

With their mission accomplished, the children bid farewell to Dino and the baby dinosaur. They stepped back into the magical portal, returning to their own time back at the Triple M Ranch in Moore, Texas.

As they lay in their beds, Justice, Teddy, Ellie, and baby Artie smiled, knowing that even in their dreams, they could travel anywhere and have incredible adventures.

"Goodnight, my brave time-traveling adventurers," whispered their grandparents as they tucked them in.

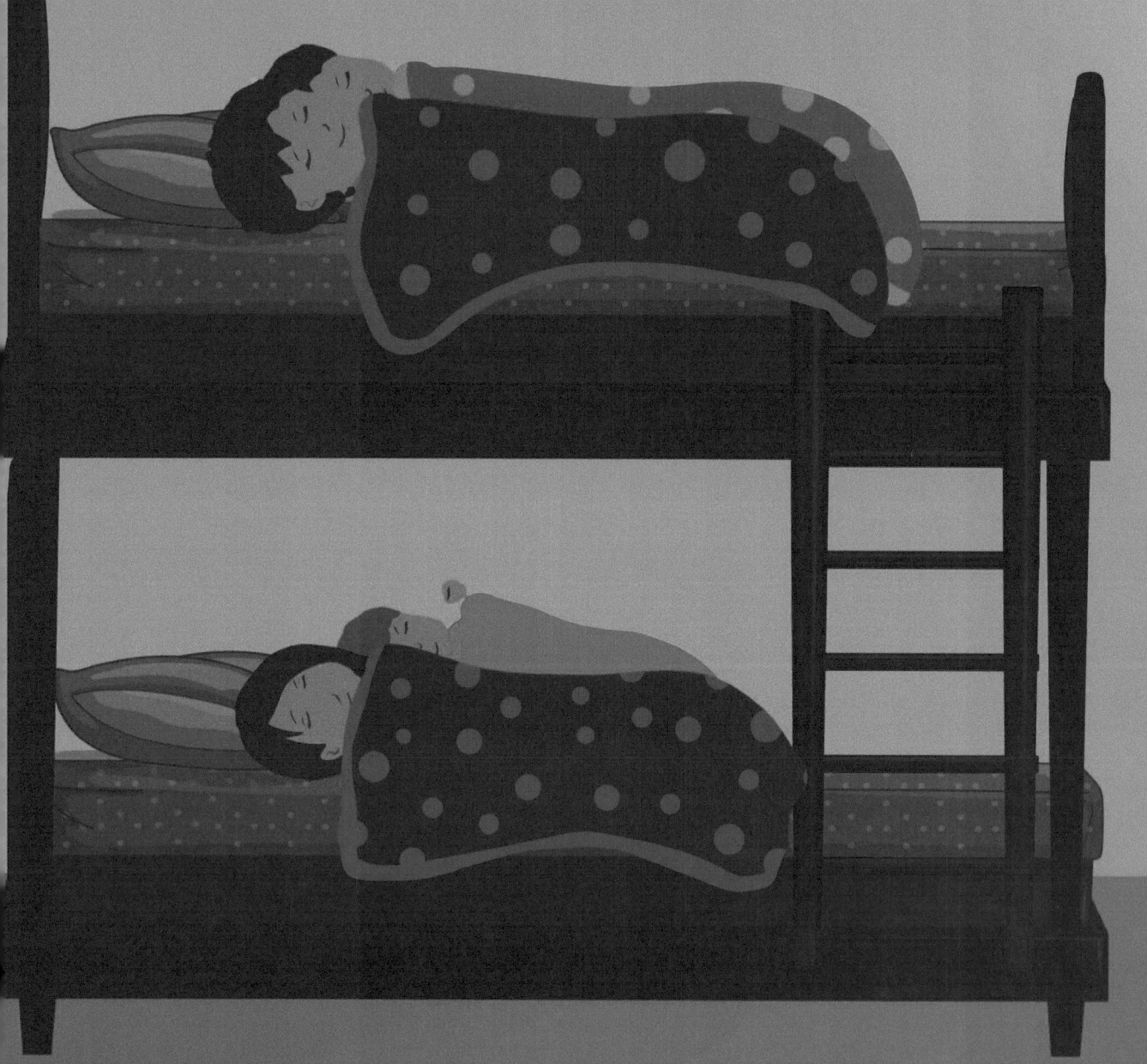

"Goodnight, Grandma Pawpaw," they replied in unison, drifting off to sleep with visions of dinosaurs dancing in their heads.

"May your dreams be filled with more wondrous adventures. Goodnight! By the way, Ellie, did you put the pocket watch up? Just checking."

"Yes, Grandma, I gave it to baby Artie, and Justice traded him a toy dinosaur for the pocket watch! Goodnight."

THE END